Max's Trip

Level 5B

Written by Melanie Hamm
Illustrated by Kate Daubney

What is synthetic phonics?

Synthetic phonics teaches children to recognise the sounds of letters and to blend (synthesise) them together to make whole words.

Understanding sound/letter relationships gives children the confidence and ability to read unfamiliar words, without having to rely on memory or guesswork; this helps them to progress towards independent reading.

Did you know? Spoken English uses more than 40 speech sounds. Each sound is called a *phoneme*. Some phonemes relate to a single letter (d-o-g) and others to combinations of letters (sh-ar-p). When a phoneme is written down it is called a *grapheme*. Teaching these sounds, matching them to their written form and sounding out words for reading is the basis of synthetic phonics.

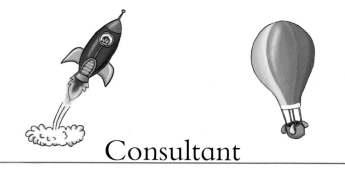

Consultant

I love reading phonics has been created in consultation with language expert Abigail Steel. She has a background in teaching and teacher training and is a respected expert in the field of synthetic phonics. Abigail Steel is a regular contributor to educational publications. Her international education consultancy supports parents and teachers in the promotion of literacy skills.

Reading tips

This book focuses on the d sound,
made with the letters ed, as in rained.

Tricky words in this book

Any words in bold may have unusual spellings or are
new and have not yet been introduced.

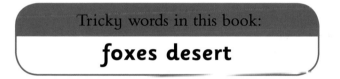

Tricky words in this book:

foxes desert

Extra ways to have fun with this book

After the reader has read the story, ask them questions
about what they have just read:

What did Max see from the hot-air balloon?
Can you remember two words that contain the
d sound shown by the letters ed?

I love holidays
and sausages!

A pronunciation guide

This grid contains the sounds used in the stories in levels 4, 5 and 6 and a guide on how to say them. /a/ represents the sounds made, rather than the letters in a word.

/ai/ as in game	/ai/ as in play/they	/ee/ as in leaf/these	/ee/ as in he
/igh/ as in kite/light	/igh/ as in find/sky	/oa/ as in home	/oa/ as in snow
/oa/ as in cold	/y+oo/ as in cube/music/new	long /oo/ as in flute/crew/blue	/oi/ as in boy
/er/ as in bird/hurt	/or/ as in snore/oar/door	/or/ as in dawn/sauce/walk	/e/ as in head
/e/ as in said/any	/ou/ as in cow	/u/ as in touch	/air/ as in hare/bear/there
/eer/ as in deer/here/cashier	/t/ as in tripped/skipped	/d/ as in rained	/j/ as in gent/gin/gym
/j/ as in barge/hedge	/s/ as in cent/circus/cyst	/s/ as in prince	/s/ as in house
/ch/ as in itch/catch	/w/ as in white	/h/ as in who	/r/ as in write/rhino

Sounds in this story are highlighted in the grid.

/f/ as in phone	/f/ as in rough	/ul/ as in pencil/hospital	/z/ as in fries/cheese/breeze
/n/ as in knot/gnome/engine	/m/ as in welcome/thumb/column	/g/ as in guitar/ghost	/zh/ as in vision/beige
/k/ as in chord	/k/ as in plaque/bouquet	/nk/ as in uncle	/ks/ as in box/books/ducks/cakes
/a/ and /o/ as in hat/what	/e/ and /ee/ as in bed/he	/i/ and /igh/ as in fin/find	/o/ and /oa/ as in hot/cold
/u/ and short /oo/ as in but/put	/ee/, /e/ and /ai/ as in eat/bread/break	/igh/, /ee/ and /e/ as in tie/field/friend	/ou/ and /oa/ as in cow/blow
/ou/, /oa/ and /oo/ as in out/shoulder/could	/i/ and /ai/ as in money/they	/c/ and /s/ as in cat/cent	/y/, /igh/ and /i/ as in yes/sky/myth
/g/ and /j/ as in got/giant	/ch/, /c/ and /sh/ as in chin/school/chef	/er/, /air/ and /eer/ as in earth/bear/ears	/u/, /ou/ and /oa/ as in plough/dough

Be careful not to add an 'uh' sound to 's', 't', 'p', 'c', 'h', 'r', 'm', 'd', 'g', 'l', 'f' and 'b'. For example, say 'fff' not 'fuh' and 'sss' not 'suh'.

Max was off on a trip.
He grabbed his bags and
his ticket.

He was so excited, he didn't even mind if it rained.

Max gave his ticket to the
pilot. He climbed into the
hot-air balloon.

"Off we go!" he called.

They hovered over the hills.
Max saw rivers and trees
and sheep.

They moved across a jungle.
Max saw tigers and lions
and snakes.

They raced over a forest.
Max saw deer and bears
and **foxes.**

In the middle of the sea,
it rained! Max saw waves and
ships and sharks.

They went to the **desert**.
Max saw sand and camels
and a rocket!

Max frowned, then shrugged.
"1, 2, 3, blast off!" yelled
the pilot.

They took off and flew to
the Moon. Max saw dust and
rocks and...

aliens!
He grabbed the pilot, "Let's go!"

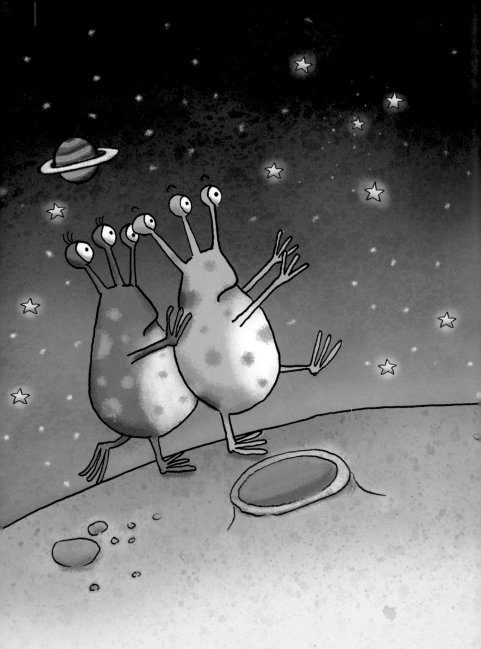

The aliens chased them back
to the rocket.

"Quick! Get inside!" cried
the pilot. He opened the door.

"Let us in!" bellowed the aliens.
"Look! We have tickets!" they
showed the pilot.

"OK," smiled the pilot.
"All aboard!"

Back at Max's house, the aliens
had dinner.

They liked it so much, they
stayed for the week!

OVER 48 TITLES IN SIX LEVELS
Abigail Steel recommends...

Some titles from Level 4

The Maze — 978-1-84898-559-9

Fairy Fay's Bad Day — 978-1-84898-560-5

Pirate School — 978-1-84898-566-7

Other titles to enjoy from Level 5

Snapped by Sam — 978-1-84898-561-2

George the Genius Gerbil — 978-1-84898-567-4

Budge Troll, Budge! — 978-1-84898-568-1

Some titles from Level 6

What Wally Wanted — 978-1-84898-563-6

Superhero Ed — 978-1-84898-564-3

The Robot Bop — 978-1-84898-570-4

An Hachette UK Company
www.hachette.co.uk

Copyright © Octopus Publishing Group Ltd 2012
First published in Great Britain in 2012 by TickTock, an imprint of Octopus Publishing Group Ltd,
Endeavour House, 189 Shaftesbury Avenue, London WC2H 8JY.
www.octopusbooks.co.uk

ISBN 978 1 84898 562 9

Printed and bound in China
10 9 8 7 6 5 4 3 2 1